# A Zebra Named Gary

# A ZEbRa NaMEd GaRY

Sámmol Hikipää & Birtá Hikipää © 2018

Published by Limelight Books
An imprint of The Write Factor
www.thewritefactor.co.uk

LIMELIGHT
BOOKS
A FOCUS ON NEW WRITING

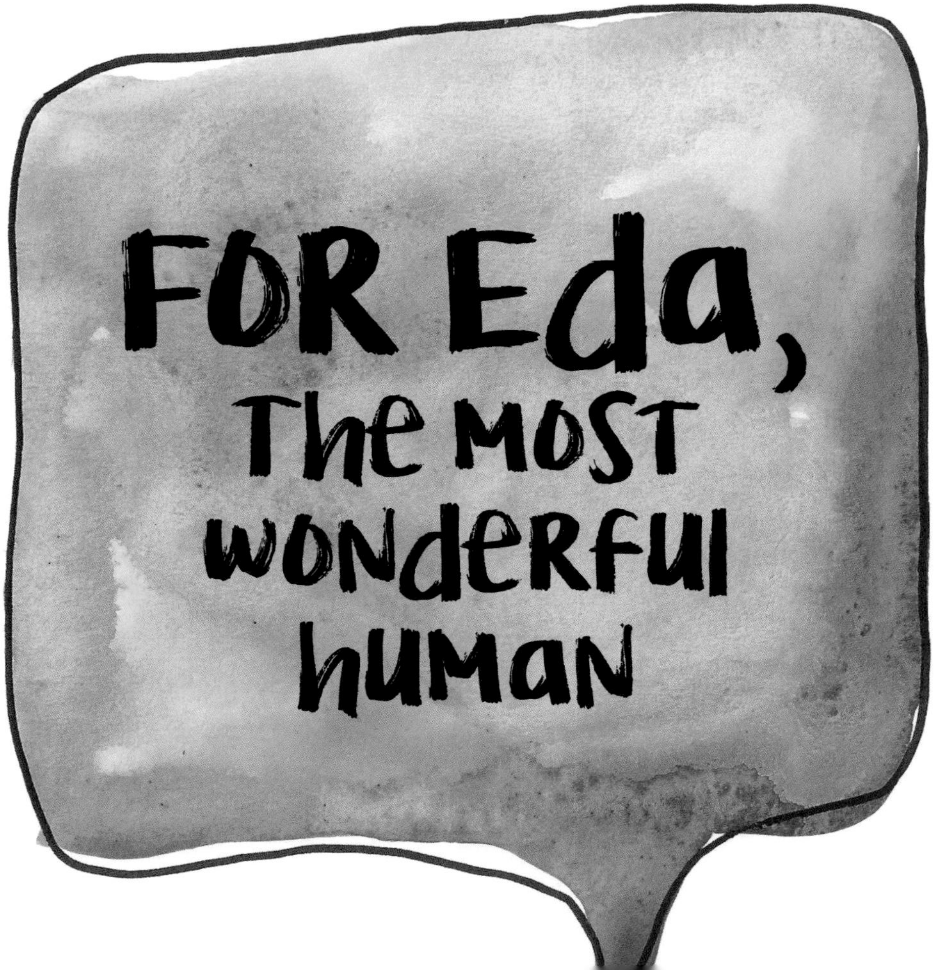
FOR Eda,
The MOST
wonderful
human

I met a
zebra called
Gary the
other day....

ANTS CAN BE ARCHITECTS

BUZZARDS CAN BE BARISTAS

# CARPS CAN be CAR MECHANICS

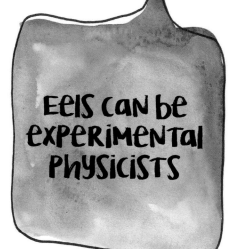

EELS CAN BE
EXPERIMENTAL
PHYSICISTS

FLAMINGOS
CAN BE
FIRE
FIGHTERS

# GOATS CAN BE GREENGROCERS

HIPPOS CAN BE HEART SURGEONS

IGUANAS CAN BE I.T. TECHNICIANS

KINGFISHERS can be kitchen fitters

LIONS can be librarians

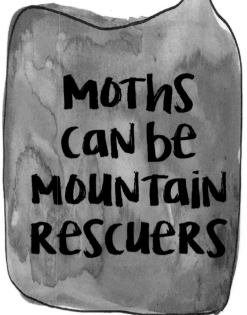

MOTHS can be MOUNTAIN RESCUERS

NEON TETRAS can be NURSES

ORCAS CAN bE OPTICIANS

PENGUINS CAN be PASTRY CHEFS

ROBINS CAN be RUGby PLAYERS

QUAILS CAN be QUARRY WORKERS

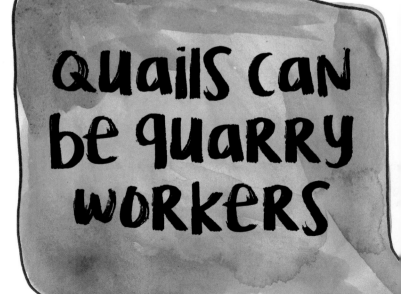

STARFISH CAN BE SECURITY GUARDS

TORTOISES CAN BE TELESALES AGENTS

# URCHINS CAN be uber drivers

VOLES CAN BE VOLUNTEER CO-ORDINATORS

WORMS CAN BE WAITERS

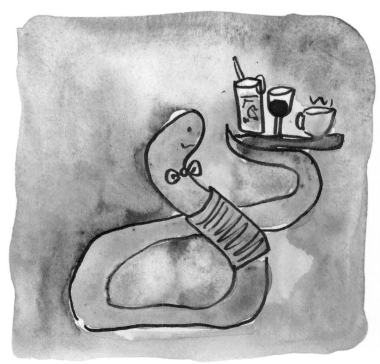

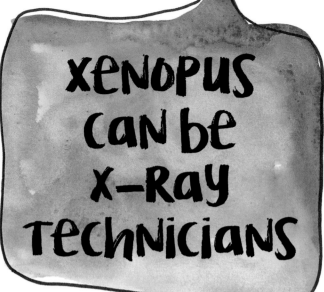

# ARE YOU a ZOO KEEPER?

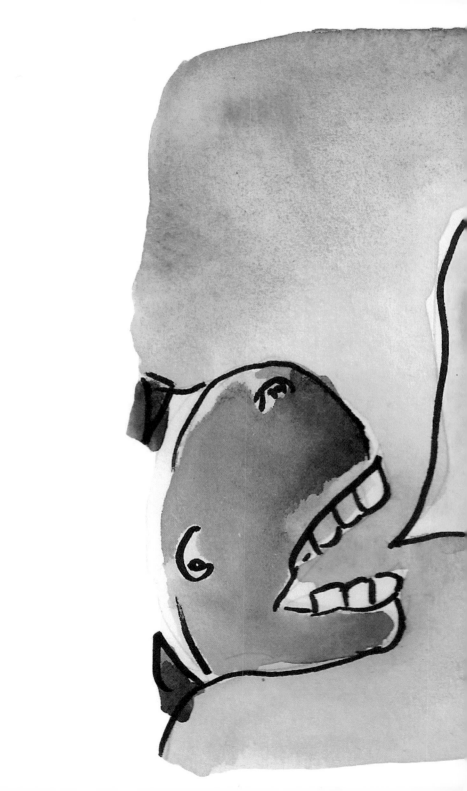

NO, I'M bETWEEN jObS AT THE MOMENT

Printed in Poland
by Amazon Fulfillment
Poland Sp. z o.o., Wrocław